MOSS-HAIRED GIRL

MOSS-HAIRED GIRL

THE CONFESSIONS
OF A CIRCUS PERFORMER
➥ BY ➥
ZARA ZALINZI
ANNOTATED BY JOSHUA CHAPMAN GREEN

A NOVELLA
R.H. SLANSKY

anvil
PRESS

ANVIL PRESS PUBLISHERS | VANCOUVER

Library and Archives Canada Cataloguing in Publication

Slansky, R. H. (Rachel H.), author
     Moss-haired girl : the confessions of a circus performer
/ R.H. Slansky.

ISBN 978-1-77214-002-6 (pbk.)

     I. Title.

PS3619.L36M67 2014   813'.6   C2014-905237-5

Printed and bound in Canada
Cover design by Derek von Essen
Interior by HeimatHouse
Represented in Canada by Publishers Group Canada and Distributed
   by Raincoast Books.
Distributed in the US by Small Press Distribution, Berkeley, CA.

The publisher gratefully acknowledges the financial assistance of the Canada
Council for the Arts, the Canada Book Fund, and the Province of British
Columbia through the BC Arts Council and the Book Publishing Tax Credit.

Anvil Press Publishers Inc.
P.O. Box 3008, Main Post Office
Vancouver, BC V6B 3X5 Canada
www.anvilpress.com

INTRODUCTION

Though my preoccupation with all things relating to circus and sideshow performers is well established, when asked how this became my field of study, I'd never had a good answer until a few years ago, when a photo album and a long-overdue library book turned up in a dark corner of my childhood home.

My brother and sister were living in London and Costa Rica, respectively, and I was travelling the U.S. researching what would become my second book, *Prodigies and Wonders: a History of the American Freakshow*. Our father had passed away several years before. We had wrestled for some time with the idea of sending our increasingly frail mother, still living in our childhood home in Columbus, Ohio, to a facility that could care for her. Unsurprisingly, she was as ambivalent about the idea as we were, so her relocation was delayed until a stroke and broken hip put her in the hospital. As soon as I heard the news, I put the book on hold and went back to Columbus. My siblings joined me as quickly as they could, and for a time we lived together again in the house in which we had grown up. The stroke had been a mild one, but the temporary paralysis complicated the hip recovery and made her vulnerable to further strokes. Unable to get out of bed and subject to temporary dementia as a side effect of recurring infections, she soon let it be known that she wasn't interested in recovery. We moved her back home for hospice care.

Before she began the process of deliberately dying, Mother insisted that we begin making claims on things we wanted from the house. This way, she would still be present to mitigate any disputes. It was an unsettling process at first, but also yielded great rewards, for, as we dug up photos and keepsakes, many of which we'd never seen, we had the opportunity to ask her about them. We learned much about her that would have been lost if those photos hadn't been found until after her death, and came to have a greater understanding of who she was and who she had been before she was our mother.

But after fifty years of accumulation, there was just more stuff than there was time, and Mother was impatient to be moving on, so by the time she stopped taking in food and water, we had hardly made a dent in it. When she died, we had only just begun to tackle the crates and boxes in the attic. Even after the service was over and she had been laid to rest, we were still coughing our way through dusty and crumbling papers and rotting ancient quilts with mysterious names embroidered on them. Eventually Leah and Ben, feeling the pull of their neglected lives abroad, cried uncle and turned over their rights to whatever remained. Ever the obsessive completist, I stayed on, digging through boxes and growing more frustrated by old unlabelled photos, the increasingly darker skins of their subjects as the years unspooled into the past the only clue that they were from my mother's side of the family, while the increasing frequency of occasional pale faces moving towards the present explained the transition to how we look today.

Then, I found a box labelled "Josh" in my own handwriting. Expecting elementary-school drawings and old airplane models, I opened it and looked upon a treasure trove I hadn't seen for more than forty years.

Mother and Dad had barely tolerated my taste in entertainment, which favoured horror comics, Raymond Chandler novels, and, of course, circus sideshows. They never went so far as to say that I was poisoning my mind with all that garbage, but their thinly veiled disgust suggested they would have been better served by a child who preferred to read Milton and take in a performance at the symphony (though they did have two other children who did just that). So one day, I packed a box with all of my most revered items, waited until Mother and Dad were having their respective evening tea and brandy in the library, then nonchalantly sauntered past, box in tow. Just as I had hoped, I was questioned. With an air of what I believed to be casual maturity, I answered that I was "just packing away some old things I had outgrown." I was nine.

I imagined that the look that passed between them was one of relief, that they had guessed at what was in the box and I had at last become a child they could be proud to call their own. From that day on, I was never seen in the house with a pulp novel or comic book. When my parents later offered to take me to the circus when it was in town (a gesture I regarded with suspicion—was I being tested?), I accepted with a blasé nod, as if it might be a lark to reminisce over my childhood interests, but I was secretly thrilled for two reasons. The first: I was going to the circus! The second: I had humbugged them! My clever ruse had not only resulted in their relaxing of their attitude toward the circus (which I would witness them enjoying, despite themselves), but I had also become free to spend many idle hours poring over my collection in the attic, free of disdain and judgement, while my professor parents taught night classes. Many evenings found me rushing down the folding stairs at the sound of their tires in the driveway gravel, brushing cobwebs from my tightly curled hair, the only visual evidence of my maternal line's origins, save for skin that tanned quickly and deeply but never seemed to burn.

Even these features could be attributed to my father's Jewish Kourlander roots, so I never thought much about them until a few years later, when a school family history project brought the truth to light. It wasn't that my parents had deliberately hidden it from us, but family history, recent or distant, was not a topic of discussion in the house unless it fell into the context of a scholarly debate. There was a sense that my parents had carried on a grand tradition of disagreeing with their parents, finding a mate who had done the same, then distancing themselves both physically and emotionally from their families of origin in adulthood, a tradition I was in the process of carrying on when Mother's hospice brought me back home again. This repeated pattern seemed explanation enough for why we rarely heard about our grandparents. One of the biggest surprises of the attic was that my mother had even kept all of those photos and artifacts for decades when she seemed so outwardly uninterested in her own history. Even my father had a stash of photos and disintegrating letters from relatives sent from ghettos and stamped by Nazi censors. Until I combed that attic, I was unaware that he had ever known any of the European family, but it turned out that he and Mother had honeymooned with them shortly before it became impossible for his aunts, uncles, and cousins to escape to America.

I opened the box and paged through each comic. I couldn't say how the stories would end as I read them, but every frame felt familiar, as though they had always remained in my memory. To my glee, I came across an issue with a story whose final frame depicting a naturalist devoured by his own collection of worm specimens had been so terrifying that I had tucked it under my brother's pillow opened to that very page. Calling to him from my upper bunk in the night, I said in my spookiest voice, "Benjamin...what's under your pillow?" The resulting scream of discovery brought Mother into the room and birthed our first brotherly conspiracy. When Mother demanded to know what had happened, after a pause, Ben said he had had a nightmare.

Because the lie saved me from getting into trouble, I felt a new respect for my brother as well as the power of the comic. It was shortly after that that I took the box to the attic. Mother continued to talk about Ben's "night terrors" well into his twenties, when we finally told her what had really happened that night. As I thumbed through that issue, I recognized the crease in that terrible page caused by Ben throwing the comic across the room after Mother had left.

I set aside the pulp novels—I would take them downstairs for a little bedside reading—and continued to thumb through crime magazines and circus programs. At the bottom of the box I found the two treasures that had formed the nucleus of my lifelong fascination.

The Civil War-era photo album was covered in peeling leather. Decades of unstable storage conditions had caused the cardboard pages to swell on either side of the ornate metal clasp, giving it a shapely waist. I unlatched it, leafing through grim-faced pictures of great-great-great-grandparents, aunts, uncles, and cousins, and puzzling over why I had stashed it in the box.

Near the back of the album I found my answer. The last four leaves held cabinet cards depicting the formal portraits of several Victorian-era sideshow performers. Now I remembered how the presence of the photos in this album had led me to the mistaken conclusion that I was related to Siamese twins, midgets, strong men, and harem girls. I had laboured under this delusion long enough to brag about it to my schoolmates before my mother set me straight by explaining that it had once been a popular pastime to collect photos of famous people. Grandpa Johnson had simply been a collector of photos, as I was a collector of baseball cards. To say I was disappointed to learn I wasn't descended from Skeleton Men and Legless Wonders would be an understatement.

In the album were two photos that struck a particularly

resonant chord of interest; one of a pale-skinned woman with an Afro in a vaguely Turkish, and for the time, scandalous costume, standing with a distinguished gentleman who sported a shock of leonine hair and brandished a conductor's wand. At their feet, a toddler in a tuxedo dressed like a miniature version of the man sat at a toy piano, his tiny hands on the keys. Below the photo their names and titles were printed: "Zara the Circassian Beauty," "Professor Hughs, the Lion of Canarvon," and "Ludwig, the Baby Beethoven." Opposite this photo in the album was another photo of what appeared to be the same woman, but with an imposing man in a vaguely Turkish costume that did little to hide his impressive physique. This photo was not labelled.

I suddenly recalled the hours spent studying these images, wondering who those people were and what the second, unlabelled photo of the woman with the other man could mean. Were the Professor and the Baby Beethoven her husband and son? Could she be their servant or a dancer in their act? Was the imposing Turk her brother? Her husband? Her captor? This mystery, coupled by the fact that the woman possessed a beauty that would hold up to our modern standards, ignited a curiosity in me that was like nothing I had ever known. But what most fascinated me was that there was something in the woman's face that felt somehow familiar, which probably helped to cement the idea in my head that the circus folk in the album must be family. In childhood, thinking I was giving her a compliment, I had showed the photo to Leah and remarked that they looked alike, but at the time she was sleeping in rollers to straighten her hair to look like the other girls at school, and took the comparison as brotherly torment.

The last item in the box would answer some of those questions, or at least purported to. It was a first-edition copy of *Moss-Haired Girl, the Confessions of a Circus Performer*, stamped with the seal of the Columbus Public Library. A small manila envelope glued to the inside of the back cover declared the book's due date: July 13, 1959. I now recalled how I had saved nearly every cent earned at my after-school job at a newsstand (what my parents knew as a bookstore). The library due date came and went, then went some more, until I had saved up enough money to approach the librarian, all contrite, and declare I simply could not locate the overdue item. One lost book replacement fee later and it was mine, and just in time, for I had been fired from the newsstand for reading comic books while people stole magazines and candy, and had lost my source of income.

In this slim volume, printed in January of 1932, just thirteen months before her death at age eighty-three (or ninety-three, according to historical documents), Zara Zalinzi herself set the record straight on the facts of her life. She spoke of the difficulties growing up the daughter of a Jewish-immigrant father and aristocratic American mother. I imagined that she felt, like I did, that though she was from two rich and established cultures, she belonged to none. The story of her life as a performer exemplified everything that enthralled me about the circus, then and now: tragedy, triumph, romance, melodrama, lucky breaks, strange and exotic people, animals, and places, and life on the road. But perhaps most important were the odd families formed by outcasts, and the blurring (and sometimes outright erasing) of the line between fact and fiction. The freedom to reinvent yourself and live amongst others who had done the same, who didn't care who you had been before. A Freak didn't have to live by the rules of "normal" society. As the family misfit, I yearned for this freedom.

Until then, I had all but forgotten Zara and her breathless and romantic account of her own life, but now that the book had fallen back into my hands, I was determined to add a chapter on her life to *Prodigies and Wonders* once I made it through all of those damn boxes and got back to the book I was supposed to be finishing.

Months of allergy medication and boxes of archival storage later, the job was finally done. The plan had been to sell the house once the contents had been distributed, but none of us seemed to be in a hurry to let it go, so we arranged for neighbours to keep an eye on it. I used the house as my home base when following leads on Zara (many sources, including herself, reported that she settled in Ohio when she retired from show business, and eventually died there), but I found little success in my searches. It seemed there were legends and anecdotes about her passed down in every tiny town in the state—even a woman descended from slaves in possession of an old *carte de visite* of Zara in costume with the word "auntie" written on the back claimed her as family, though she couldn't say exactly how they were connected. Nothing led to the establishment of concrete fact. This was not uncommon in researching circus folk—obviously, that's a large element of what drew me to the subject to begin with. But, for some reason, maybe because I had identified with Zara so strongly, coupled with the fact that I had lost my chance to know more about my own origins when Mother died with all the answers, I needed to know the truth about Zara Zalinzi.

The publishing deadline loomed for *Prodigies and Wonders* and I still didn't have enough research to merit a full chapter on Zara. Reluctantly, I had to concede to my wife's suggestion that she might not make the cut and swapped in another Circassian Beauty, Imza Adzel, in her stead. The book went to print and did well enough that I was offered another contract. My obsession-addled brain went wild at the thought of making the subject Zara, but Jane, my wise and patient wife, suggested I break from the world of the circus and take a pass at something, *anything* else of interest. At that point, I could hardly recall having any prior interests until she reminded me that, just before my mother's stroke, I had made acquaintance with Mort Bell, the very artist who had pencilled the image in the horror comic that I had used to terrorize my brother. Mort was well-advanced in years and in erratic health, so if I was to make him a subject I'd best get started sooner rather than later. Thanks to my wife, and not for the first time, my balance was restored. I set up camp in Chicago in order to be closer to Mort.

While I was interviewing Mort and other former comic-industry folks and their descendants for what would become *Ghouls! Creeps! Fiends!: How Horror Comics Changed Suburban America*, Jane took a phone call from a childhood friend of mine in Ohio. He said he had come across an obituary in the newspaper that mentioned that the deceased had been the granddaughter of circus performers—a former harem girl and a Circassian prince, and, remembering my obsession with Zara, wanted to pass the info along. Fearing, and rightly so, that this new development might send me off the rails, Jane asked the friend to scan and email a copy of the obituary to her. While she didn't want me to lose sight of my current goal, she didn't want the lead to grow cold, either, so she took a sick day to attend the funeral herself. There she met the only living child of the deceased, Sarah M., who was named for her great-grandmother, Zara Zalinzi, and was the daughter of the grandchild who took Zara in during her declining years. Sarah M., a diagnosed agoraphobe, was more than willing to speak to my wife (and myself, once *Ghouls! Creeps! Fiends!* was completed), but out of respect for her condition and the rift created in her family as Zara's true origins became clear, her full name and the names of her family members have been either withheld or changed.

When Jane finally told me what she had been up to, the first thing she did was hand me the now well-known photo that would hold the key to unlocking the truth behind Zara's biggest humbug: her own identity.

And now, Ladies and Gentlemen, without further ado, may I present to you, Zara Zalinzi, the Moss-Haired Beauty, Circassian Princess, and former Harem Slave, in her own words![1]

And so the story begins...

[1] Annotated with findings from my research.

CHAPTER ONE

I ENTER THE WORLD—THE PAUPER AND THE HEIRESS—A SERIOUS DEBATE UNRESOLVED—A STOW-AWAY—MY FIRST GLIMPSE OF THE CIRCUS

I was born, not in a palace in the Circassian Mountains, but in a plain but cozy cabin in Virginia, not far from Leesylvania, in December of 1850. My mother, Gabrella, had been a member of the illustrious and long-established Lee family and was set to marry a cousin in a month. On one excursion into town, she met my father, Solomon, a Jew who had recently come from Latvia, where he had been a practicing physician.[2]

---

[2] Zara appears to start out her confession with at least one fabrication. Though her deliberate omission of her parents' respective surnames (and nearly all proper names throughout this book) makes it difficult to confirm, it appears that there were no births to any free people named Solomon and Gabrella or any possible variants from 1830-1860 in the state of Virginia, which then encompassed what is now West Virginia. There were, however, four births (one of which died in infancy) and two stillbirths to a Sal and Gaby Selinsky in Ohio between 1833 and 1845. In one of these birth records was what I initially overlooked as a mistake by the clerk because it didn't match the others: Gaby's race is listed as "M," for mulatto. It wasn't until I came into contact with Sarah M. that I began to consider the possibility that only that one record had been correct. If so, Solomon had married and raised children with a runaway slave.

Zara also gives her birth year as 1850 here, but various records contradict this (making her older), and even Zara seems to get confused; compared against the historical dates of the events she describes, her age fluctuates in relation to her declared birth year, even throughout this book.

Unable to find work in America in his field, Father was eking out a living as a travelling peddler. Despite his lowly occupation, he seemed a happy man. Quite well-educated, he spoke English fluently, as well as Greek, Latin, and Spanish, and could play every instrument for sale on his cart with great skill. Within minutes of meeting his acquaintance, my mother, who had had an unusual amount of education for the time and was also a gifted musician, knew she couldn't marry her cousin, who was a military man with little interest in matters of culture.

Mother came to her parents to confess her change of heart. Solomon had asked to marry her and she was hoping for their blessing. Instead, she was given an ultimatum—marry her cousin or she was no longer their daughter. Mother stood her ground— she felt she must follow her heart if she were to live her life in happiness. Her father threw her out on the spot, not even allowing her to pack a bag.[3]

As she descended the grand porch, in tears, for the last time, Solomon, who had been waiting outside in the hopes he would be invited in to meet his future in-laws, could see that the outcome was unfavourable. Unable to bear the thought that she would lose her family over him, he tried to convince her to change her mind, but she was resolute. As they were climbing into his cart to steal away into the night, from the plantation house came a hoarse whisper. Grandmother had snuck away in the night to say goodbye. She bade my mother not to forget them. Through

---

[3] The Lee line has been exhaustively researched by generations of descendants. No record has yet been found of this engagement and its subsequent dissolution, a scandal that would have likely made its way into lore in a family so large, prominent, and intermarried. This seems to support my theory that this was an elaborate fabrication to cover up a much more painful truth.

her tears, my mother promised she would think of them every day, and, though she rarely spoke of it, I am certain she kept that promise. She was very close to Grandmother and it pained her acutely to know she would likely never see her again. She was not so close to her father, who treated her with cruelty while coddling her other siblings,[4] but over time she forgave him, and even grew to cherish his memory.

Off into the night fled my mother and father. Mother was exhausted from her ordeal, so they stopped for the night to sleep in a barn. Father made a bed of straw for her and began to make another for himself, but Mother said that, as far as she was concerned, they were as good as married already, so there was no need for modesty—they could share one bed of straw, and did.[5]

They woke before dawn and moved on, before they could be discovered.

My eldest sister was born nine months later. By that time, father had saved enough profit to rent a one-room cabin. In that cabin was next born another sister, who did not survive the birth, then another who did, then a brother. That brother had a go of

---

[4] This could be evidence in support of the idea that he was not her natural father. More on that later.

[5] No marriage record has yet been found for this union. This could be due to the fact that the reporting of births, marriages, and deaths to authorities was still voluntary at that time, but it is also possible that the marriage was never made legal. If Gabrella's mother was indeed a slave, according to law, Zara was also considered one at birth. It is easily understandable that a runaway slave might not want to bring herself to the attention of any authorities. Even in a free state, and Ohio was a free territory that became a free state, bounty hunters roamed the land in search of the handsome reward that a runaway slave could bring.

it,[6] for after him were born three more girls, me being the last; the one before me also did not survive.[7]

That poor dear had been given the name of my grandmother, which had been originally intended for the previous babe who had also died. When the second sister did not live to possess the name, Mother bestowed it upon me against the wishes of Father, who, in keeping with his religious customs, did not believe it prudent to name a child at birth, particularly a name with a jinx upon it. But the third time was apparently the charm, for I was a healthy and vibrant child and the apple of my father's eye.

By the time of my birth, the cabin had grown to three small but cozy rooms. All was well within our home, but outside of it, things were different. Though Father wasn't devout, as a Jew in a small Virginia village he was treated poorly. For Mother and we children, it was much of the same—she was looked down upon for marrying him and we were pitied as half-breeds; other parents kept their children from becoming our playmates. Because of this, we siblings grew very close. As it became increasingly difficult and unpleasant for Father to peddle his wares, he began to discuss the possibility of relocating the family to the city through correspondence with a brother who had established himself there.[8]

---

[6] Zara never uses the given names of any of her siblings.

[7] This scrambled account of the births of her siblings, their birth order and sex, as well as the stillbirths, lines up with the birth records of the Sal and Gaby Selinsky in Ohio.

[8] Here, again, Zara is frustratingly vague. Which city? The evidence (such as it is) seems to point to Manhattan. There were several adult male Hebrew Selinskys (or various spelling variations thereof) born in Russia, what Latvia was often referred to at the time, living in Manhattan in this time period of the right age to be Solomon's brother, but since there are no records in the

Mother was conflicted. The city seemed an unsafe place to raise children, but our position in the community caused her to despair of our little family ever finding happiness or comfort. Perhaps in a large-enough city we might find ourselves only one of many different kinds of people? While Mother and Father debated the issue, a letter came from my uncle alerting my father that a museum owner from the city would soon be coming through with his travelling show.[9]

If my father had any curiosities to sell, this man would be interested in procuring them and would pay a fair price. My uncle, who was the Showman's supplier of feed for his museum menagerie,[10] had already spoken of my father to the man, so he could consider himself introduced.

As my uncle knew, my father was a collector of curiosities, and had been since prior to his immigration. People for miles around knew he would take two-headed turtles and Indian arrowheads off their hands for a few coins, items that were useless to them otherwise. Together with a local embalmer and taxidermist, father had prepared and amassed a collection that spilled from his peddler's cart to the house and drove my mother to distraction. Well I can recall her complaining of the pressure

---

U.S. to tie Solomon to any family members beyond his own nuclear family, Manhattan must be considered speculative.

[9] Again, very vague, but if Manhattan is correct we can narrow the identity of the showman down to three people, the mostly likely of them being the illustrious H.R. Putnam himself.

[10] All records at Putnam's Museum of Wonders were destroyed by fire, making confirmation that a Selinsky was ever a vendor for the museum an impossibility.

of preparing dinner beneath the single, staring eye of the Cyclops Goat head in a jar on the kitchen shelf. To my eyes, all of the poor things were as precious little angels, too special for this earth. I treasured each and wondered if, had they but lived long enough to become my pets, they might have made me feel less alone. Having known the judging stares of strangers who looked down upon my parentage, I felt a kindred spirit to these sweet little beasts.

My father sensed an opportunity for more than just a one-time transaction—he had a mind for this showman to come to think of him as a regular supplier. He kept a keen ear and eye for any sign of the showman's arrival, but needlessly so, for soon there were full-page ads disguised as articles in every local paper and handbills plastered to every post for miles around declaring the wonders and marvels that were soon to descend upon us. A marvellous menagerie and countless curiosities were described, as well as a seemingly endless list of performers, each more outrageous than the last—a show to end all shows that we would never forget. Everyone for miles around was abuzz with curiosity and it seemed the travelling show was the only topic of discussion. As opening day approached, I begged my father to take me with him, but Mother was dubious at the prospect, for it seemed I would be subjected to much more sensational sights than a seven-year-old girl should ever see.[11]

My oldest sister had recently married at the tender age of sixteen, and the next oldest had gone away to be a live-in maid for a wealthy family.[12]

---

[11] Here Zara either misremembers or fudges her age, for if she is Sarah Selinsky, she would have been thirteen.

[12] The 1860 census, taken approximately two years after the travelling show came through town, finds the Ohio Selinskys diminished to only Gaby and

My brother, who had become my only companion at home, had been deemed old enough to attend. This seemed a great injustice to me as he was older only by five years. I was to stay at home beside my mother—that was her decree.

On the day of the big show, the excitement all around had reached a fever pitch. My father, having combed his collection of oddities for the most unusual items to present to the Showman for sale, including a concoction fabricated by the taxidermist and himself from the skins of a large bird and wild cat—the "Athenian Siren" that was to become so famous—hooked the horses to the cart in the early morning light. Understanding my devastation at being barred from the show, my brother was especially kind to me and promised to bring back something as a keepsake.

But I had already determined to see the show with my own eyes. By the time Father took the reins of the cart and my brother trotted alongside it, trundling his hoop before him, I had secured myself within, the Siren in my lap. As I bumped and swayed amid bottles of pickled twinned piglets and deformed baby chicks, I became aware of the sounds and smells of the show before we were near enough to see the big white tents—the trumpeting of elephants, a lion's roar, the smells of the menagerie, sweet caramel, and roasted sausage links. When at last the cart came to a stop and Father unlatched the door to present his wares to the Showman, he found me there, frozen in fear to find both him and the finely dressed Showman gazing back.

---

a boy named Jake (relationships between household members were not noted in U.S. Census records until 1880). If this is the right family, this would support the idea that two of the girls were no longer at home and another may have died in childhood. My attempts to locate the two oldest daughters in census and vital records were unsuccessful.

"Well, that is a curiosity, indeed," said the famous man with a twinkle in his eye. I knew his likeness from every handbill and poster and advert. "Surely the most life-like doll I have ever laid eyes on! How much are you asking for that marvel?"

When Father had recovered from his astonishment, he shooed me away and bade my brother wander the show with me and not let me out of his sight. I was taken by the hand and reluctantly led away from the Showman, but his warmth and humour had made an indelible impression upon me and I hoped against hope I would have a chance to meet him again.[13]

---

[13] Putnam was renowned for his good nature and sense of fun, one of many reasons to conclude he was the Showman in question.

CHAPTER TWO

A SERIOUS DEBATE RESOLVED—ESCAPE TO THE BIG
CITY—A CURIOUS BIRTH—A ROYAL VISIT—A TERRI-
BLE LOSS—A BITTERSWEET REMINDER

Father's first meeting with the Showman went better than he could have ever dreamed. He was paid more than fairly for the items he sold, which was everything he had brought, including, to my mother's relief, the Cyclops Goat. The Showman instantly saw that the Athenian Siren was humbug, but could not see exactly how it had been fabricated; the animal was so cleverly crafted. He was eager to put it before the public and see their reaction,[14] and extended an invitation for my father to contact him if he found himself in possession of any more unexplainable curiosities. My father, a bit of a showman in his own right, did not reveal he had only sold the Showman a fraction of his extensive collection.

At the end of the day, my father collected my brother and me, both exhausted but buzzing with excitement over the wonders we had seen. Father drove home in the twilight and we fell asleep in the now-empty cart, dreaming of beautiful ladies in tights balancing on horseback, herds of tamed elephants dancing in formation, and giantesses holding midgets in hand as if they were living dolls.

---

[14] Though not so well known as the Sumatran Seamaid humbug, accounts of the controversial exhibition of the Siren have survived. Alas, images of the creature have not.

The money Father brought home and the offer made by the Showman to purchase future wares removed all remaining doubt from my mother's head on the subject of moving to the city. Suddenly it seemed to her just the place to begin life anew. By morning it had been decided, and by month's end arrangements had been made and our belongings were packed up.[15]

My two sisters, the eldest of whom was with her first child, made a final visit, challenging my mother's resolve somewhat at the prospect of being farther removed from them. But even they agreed it was a shrewd course of action, and promised to come and visit once we had settled.[16]

Father had rented a wagon large enough to hold all our possessions, but it was fortunate that the size of our home had kept their number so humble. As Father and Mother steered the wagon, my brother drove Father's cart behind, me at his side.

---

[15] The fact that the timeline suggests the family moved to the city in 1858 but Gaby and Jake still appear in Ohio in the 1860 census has two possible explanations. Either the move to the city did not happen so spontaneously, or Solomon may have taken Zara ahead and sent for his wife and son once established. The former supposition would also explain why Sal and Sarah Selinsky do not appear in the census record with Gaby and Jake. I have been unable to locate Solomon and Zara in New York or elsewhere for that census year.

[16] This is the last mention of either of these siblings, but probably not the last Zara saw of them. Before Sarah M. and the photo turned up, I had been contacted by a woman named Wilma, who had found a *carte de visite* of Zara in costume between the leaves of an old book that had belonged to her grandfather. On the reverse someone had written the word "auntie." Looking for more information on Zara, Wilma came across my book, *Prodigies and Wonders*, which mentioned Zara in passing in the chapter on Circassian Beauty, Imza Adzel. This prompted her to send a letter to my publisher with

Along the road, people came out to watch our caravan, disappointed by its size and ordinary occupants after the scale and wonder of the Circus Day procession that had come through earlier in the month.

After a brief stay in my uncle's family's small apartment we were soon able to move into our own, even smaller apartment. My father quickly built his reputation as a man in search of curiosities, and the Showman occasionally stopped by the small storefront Father had rented to select items from his collection. My brother worked in the store and Mother took up piecework to supplement our income. I was soon at work beside her. Much to her dismay, I had acquired an emaciated stray cat who quickly grew fat and was often curled up beside me as I crafted my silk flowers.

---

a photocopy enclosed of her grandfather's picture of his "auntie," and though it was not a high-resolution image, it was clearly a picture of Zara. Excited by the possibility of a breakthrough and unbeknownst to Jane, who was doing her best to keep me on track with *Ghouls! Creeps! Fiends!*, I called Wilma, but it turned out we were both in the same boat for that first talk—with a dearth of information and the fervent hope that the other had all the answers we were seeking. Wilma hadn't done any research into documentation of her family history, but their oral history sounded like the typical American tall tale—a royal ancestor here, a slave there, a war hero or two, and an outlaw just to keep it interesting. Thinking of the assumptions I had made about the circus folks in my own family album, I suggested to Wilma the possibility that the photo of Zara in her family keepsakes might be responsible for the legend of Turkish slaves in her family, and she corrected me to say that the slaves had not been Turkish, but African American. It was too much of a mess with too little documentation, and we ended the call, both discouraged. But when the book was done and Jane presented me with Sarah M.'s photo, Wilma's story, however undocumented historically, suddenly seemed worth revisiting. I left Chicago to meet with her that weekend, and was surprised to discover that Wilma was black.

[25]

One day, the cat crawled beneath my bed, where she yowled and would not come out, no matter how I entreated her. When Father came home he moved the bed aside and revealed that my dear puss has not grown fat after all; five kittens squirmed blindly beside the proud new mama. Leaning close, I saw that she had found her true family when she followed me home, for suckling at her breast along with his brethren was a striped-gray tabby with two sweet little heads.

Father wasted no time in getting the curious kitten and myself into the cart and to the museum. I tucked the creature in my jacket to keep her warm. Soon I was before the Showman once again, shyly saying hello.

"How wonderful it is that your doll can talk!" the Showman remarked to my father, eyes twinkling with mischief. "And what have you brought me, little Sarah?" he asked.[17]

Since we had last spoken, she had done some family research and turned up a memoir and family tree full of inaccuracies written by her great-great grandmother Dora, whose maiden name was … Selitsky. (Until the age of the Social Security Administration in America, spellings varied fairly frequently and less care was taken with official records to be sure there were no mistakes, so the "t" where the "n" should be was of little consequence.) In her memoir, Dora spoke of her parents moving to the city after she had married young, and visiting them before their early deaths in their small home with her husband and children. Though she mentioned having sisters and a brother early in the memoir, Dora made no mention of them in connection with these visits. However, in one of many anecdotes illustrating the imagination of her eldest son, who eventually became a well-respected artist, Dora briefly relates that he once came home from the circus claiming he had seen his auntie in the sideshow. Wilma, the direct descendant of this son, produced the original cabinet card of Zara with the word "auntie" inscribed on the reverse. Things were beginning to come together.

I reached inside my jacket for the kitten, but then burst into tears, for the poor thing had died on the way. The Showman knelt to comfort me.

"There, there," he said, offering up a clean cotton handkerchief from his pocket.

I was humiliated, feeling myself much too old for this display, but somehow the sight of that poor creature in eternal stillness was too much for me to bear. The Showman conferred with my father, their voices low, then asked if I would like to see the menagerie. I tearfully accepted his offer. There followed a personal tour of the most prized collection of exotic animals on earth with the great Showman himself. By the tour's end I had quite collected myself and so charmed him with my knowledge of the creatures therein, that he offered me a job as a ticket girl that paid double in a day what I would have earned for piecework in a week. Fearing I might lose the opportunity were the offer to be proposed to my parents, I accepted on the spot. Once again returned to my father, who had stayed behind to arrange for the preservation of the kitten, I announced to him the news of my gainful employment, which was met with surprise and, thankfully, acceptance. By this time I had all but forgotten about the kitten, but I would see my dear puss again in a few weeks— stuffed and mounted and looking no worse for the wear on a shelf in the Cabinet of Curiosities.[18]

---

[17] It was this singular mention of Zara's given name that made me wonder if the clue to finding her true identity could be so obvious. Zara; Sarah. Could her actual last name be the basis for her pseudonym? I returned to the census and birth records looking for sound-alikes for Zalinzi, and that's when the Selinskys started to turn up.

Much has been made of the visit to the museum made by the young British Prince.[19]

Until now, in order to preserve my Circassian identity, I have never confessed that I was there to witness it. The Showman was out of town on that day, but sent word that I would be performing my first humbug. I, a cheeky little American girl, was to demand a ticket from the Prince at the museum entrance as if he were any ordinary patron. By then I was already familiar with the Showman's sense of humour and the pleasure he took in pulling a leg, and knew there was no ill will in the plan. I have even wondered if his very absence was a good-natured ribbing of the monarch to demonstrate that we in the colonies don't take royalty so seriously. I, however, confess to a great deal of anticipation on my part. Much attention was paid to my appearance on that day, and my lines were rehearsed again and again. I was as nervous as I had ever been.

When the time came for my first performance, the museum was closed to the public to ensure the Prince's safety. First through the doors to the lobby, where I waited, came his guards,

---

[18] This kitten does not appear in any printed materials or recollections of *Putnam's Cabinet of Curiosities*, a collection whose items numbered in the tens of thousands over its decades in existence. Because the museum and the collection within was destroyed by fire and rebuilt twice, a complete inventory has not survived. A vintage polycephalic taxidermy kitten that was alleged to have been part of Putnam's museum collection did turn up in an antique store in New Jersey in the 1970s, but was subsequently sold, and is now lost.

[19] In 1860, the Prince of Wales became the first British monarch to set foot on American soil. Putnam's museum was one of many uniquely American destinations on his itinerary.

looking stately in their pressed and spotless uniforms. Next came the manager of the museum, who was filling in as ambassador for the Showman. When at last the guest of honour made his appearance and proceeded to the inner doors, I stepped in front to bar the way.

"Ticket, please," said I. The Prince looked down, astonished at the impertinence of this little American girl. A moment that seemed an eternity followed, wherein his handlers seemed at a loss for what to do. They looked to the manager, who looked evenly at the Prince.

"You did purchase a ticket, did you not?" the manager asked.

The Prince looked down at my outstretched and waiting hand, a little bit of improvisation. I struggled to keep my expression stone-faced, a worry that I could be a party to a diplomatic incident beginning to form in my mind.

His Royal Highness suddenly laughed, and nervous giggles at last escaped me. The Prince took my outstretched hand, turned it over, and placed a chivalrous kiss upon the back of it as the manager at last chuckled while the guards and handlers politely applauded the show.

"Charming girl," he murmured, then proceeded with the manager through the grand inner doors of the museum. Though I was but a young girl,[20] the kiss from the young Prince made an

---

[20] If Zara is Sarah Selinsky, she would have been fifteen or sixteen during this incident, if it happened at all, and only two or three years younger than the Prince of Wales, who was nineteen at the time of his American visit. All other historical accounts of the Prince's visit do not include this anecdote, which doesn't mean that it was a fabrication, but it does seem like the kind of story that Putnam would have enjoyed relating in one of his many autobiographical sketches.

impression upon me that I did not fully understand at the time. I had yet to feel my heart stir for a member of the opposite sex, but I had begun to notice the effect my presence had on them.

I worked at the museum as a ticket girl as well as in various other capacities for some time, and in so doing, made the acquaintance of the various performers in residence. Though I was not possessed of any deformities or unusual talents, they were quite welcoming to me. Many of them became lifelong friends, a giantess and an armless woman in particular.[21]

I helped to dress the Aztec Twins before performances and soaked the hair of the Circassian Beauty in stale beer.[22]

---

[21] Mabel Birch, a 7-foot 9-inch pathologically shy woman with a great sensitivity about the size of her feet, was a member of Putnam's company. When she died in Ohio in 1889, she was buried in a steel casket and had the grave poured with concrete so that her body would lay undisturbed by the curious.

The best candidate for the armless woman is almost certainly Fanny Armbruster (her actual given name), who wore trousers under her skirts for modesty in order to lift her teacup to her mouth with her toes. A collection of Fanny's belongings donated to an Ohio museum upon her death includes two letters from an old and dear friend "Sarah" who was a retired and widowed circus performer living nearby. The donated items also included several images of Zara Zalinzi in costume with cryptic personal messages on the back. The letters from "Sarah" indicate they were written with great frequency but only the two have surfaced thus far.

[22] A large rotating cast of women performed as Circassian Beauties for Putnam, but Imza Adzel and Luza Lola, the only two documented resident Circassian performers in the period before the first fire, are the most likely candidates to have had Zara as a hairdresser.

I was taught chess by the Showman's most prized performer, a midget who sometimes took a full day of thought to make a single move upon the board.[23]

I had tea with the ferocious-looking but tremendously polite Tattooed Man and played at Jacks with the albino children. About the only people I could not become friendly with were the Bearded Lady and the Strongman, who were billed as a couple but seemed to barely be able to stand each other away from the lights of the stage. The Bearded Lady was ever cross and viewed my offers to tend to her child, a beautiful little girl with not a trace of her mother's affliction, so that she might rest, with suspicion. The Strong Man seemed to prefer brooding to discourse, so I left him to himself despite my curiosity about him.[24]

---

[23] Putnam's star attraction, little person Admiral Jim Ferrell, was known for carrying chess games out for weeks.

[24] Madame Anya, by all accounts born normal, had reason to be cranky. After the difficult birth of her first child, she began to grow a beard. The doctors attempted to keep this development from her during her long recovery from childbirth, ordering all mirrors in the house covered, but her husband spied an opportunity for financial gain. He presented her with her own image and, as the story goes, as she was reeling from the shock, suggested they charge money for people to ogle her. When she refused, he turned against her. She divorced him, gaining custody of the child. Eventually she found herself unable to make ends meet and contacted Putnam herself, to go on display. At least she had the satisfaction of knowing that her former husband wouldn't share in her profits when she boarded at the museum with her child.

Ivan the Great is less documented, but unlabelled photos survive of him and Anya posing together, suggesting they were indeed billed as a couple. Ivan, a supposed Russian in Siberian exile who was rescued by sympathetic natives from his prison duties of felling trees for lumber with a single blow

Though I remember these days at the museum with much fondness, a black cloud was hanging over us all in the form of the War Between the States.

During this time, my brother became unable to ignore the call of his country. Against the tearful remonstrations of my mother, he volunteered for service. By the year's end, we had received word that he had perished in battle. Mother was inconsolable.[25]

---

of his fist and ice-fishing with his bare hands when his captors had run out of bait, wore a fur loincloth and not much else to direct attention to his impressive physique and away from the easily crushed balsa wood and aluminum props that stood in for oak and steel. One anecdote has it that a native Russian once called out to him from the audience to test his story with an insult so vile that no Russian could have refrained from responding. Ivan's expression did not even flicker. Soon after, a warning to the audience to not address Ivan directly was added to his introductory spiel, for his strength was such that he could break free from his chains (also added to the act) and the management could not be responsible for his actions. Though his native language has never been positively confirmed (at least not officially, despite his apparent later connection to Zara and her claims of his origins), it seems safe to assume that it wasn't Russian.

[25] In my initial research, searches of Civil War soldiers yielded more than one male Selinsky, or spelling variant thereof, none of whom could be tied conclusively to the family of Sarah Selinsky. Thanks to Wilma's research, we now know that his given name was Jacob and his mother's maiden name was Wilson. On a whim, I searched for Jake Wilson in the soldier's records. With a name that common I came up with an unmanageable number of candidates, so I narrowed it down to New York enlistees. There were fourteen, but only one who died on the field. That Jake Wilson was a member of the U.S. Colored Troops. His service records are brief and contain no identifying information that could tie him to Zara's family, though they do

It was soon after that that an envelope arrived, sent from the town she had fled from with Father to begin their lives together. In it was a photo of her own parents, the grandparents I had never known. It gave her a shock to see how they had aged in the years since she had left, but it also consoled her that her mother, in whose hand the envelope was addressed, still thought enough of her to secretly post the picture to her and to help her keep up her promise to never forget.

Many were the times I found her sitting in her chair, gazing upon that photograph, the subjects of which I could not see from my viewpoint and so imagined the appearance of many times over. If ever I tried to catch a glimpse of it, it would be tucked into her pocket by the time I came near and she would have forced herself to shake free her melancholy. I have that photo beside me as I write.[26]

---

indicate that the Jake in question was sent home for burial in Ohio. The majority of Wilma's family has been buried for generations in the same cemetery, and there is a J. Wilson in the midst of them who died in 1865 at age twenty-five (the right age to be Jake Selinsky). Per Wilma, no one in the family knows how this J. Wilson fits into the family buried around him. But Wilson is a family name, and the marker does not distinguish its denizen as a Civil War veteran, so it remains a rather hopeful and romantic leap of imagination to suppose Jake took on his mother's name, reclaimed her race, and joined up to fight for the freedom of other African Americans. There is no reason to believe he knew anything about his mother's true origins, but if he did, it's possible that it was no secret in the household and Zara knew and hid it all along. Still, imagining Jake's transformation as he watches the war unfold, hears of the formation of the Colored Troops regiment, then joins up with them under the surname of his slave ancestors rather than using his father's surname to join a white regiment, is deeply stirring.

[26] This is almost certainly the photo given to my wife by Sarah M. Per Sarah, during her mother's childhood visits with Zara, she would often look up from playing to see Zara staring at the photo. Zara told Sarah's mother that they were her own grandparents and that, though she had never met them herself, she had seen her own mother take out the photo once a day to consider it, so she did so, too. Zara's claim that she had only seen the back of the photo until her mother's death would support the idea that even she had little sense of her true origins until her adulthood. When I met with Wilma in person that first time, I was amazed to discover that she had turned up another copy of the same photo after finding a distant cousin searching for the same family online. The cousin had no idea how or even if it fit into their family history. On the back of that photo someone had inscribed in crude handwriting the words, "Love, Mother."

CHAPTER THREE

A DEVASTATING FIRE—MOTHER TAKES TO BED—
BIGGER AND BETTER—A CHANGE OF CAREER—
A LION TAKES A BRIDE—MOTHERLESS CHILD—
A CHILD BECOMES A MOTHER

One morning, I arrived at the breakfast table to find Mother and Father whispering over the front page of the newspaper. Father informed me in a sombre tone that there had been a terrible fire at the museum. Fearing the worst for my dear friends who resided there, tears immediately sprang to my eyes, but my parents were quick to assure me that all had been rescued before the flames had engulfed the building. But of my beloved animals, however, few had survived, mostly exotic birds that had flown away into the dark night.[27]

I was suddenly without employ. Again, I took up piecework at the side of my mother, who was still reeling from the loss of my brother. Her sorrow was impossible to lift and, I selfishly admit, difficult for me to bear. I desperately missed the lively folks I had grown so accustomed to seeing every day at the museum, all of whom had met with tragedy in their lives but had turned their pain into their fortune and met each day as if it was meant to be lived. Here in the small apartment with my mourning mother, I felt sure the pain of my brother's loss would drown us both, as if it were a poison seeping from her sighing breast into my own.

---

[27] A fire destroyed Putnam's museum in 1861. It was a total loss in terms of property and nearly all of the animals perished, but firemen went to heroic measures to rescue all the human inhabitants, even using a crane to free the resident fat lady, whose bulk could not fit through any usable exits.

One day, Mother rose heavily from her chair to check the supper roast and fainted dead away. I managed to get her into bed and place a cool cloth on her brow, but she claimed she was merely overtired from late nights before the gas lamp, and refused to allow me to call for a physician. When Father came home from the shop he would brook no such nonsense, and the doctor was there in a flash.[28]

Nervous exhaustion was the diagnosis, and rest was the treatment. Now that Father, who refused to hire help, was running the shop alone, I was Mother's caretaker during the day. I could not leave her alone even long enough to run to the corner for some sugar, for I would return to find she had attempted some task and lay helpless in a heap upon the floor. I took over the piecework for the both of us, but the money was meagre in comparison to my former wages at the museum. The doctor made several expensive return calls, tipping the scales on which our finances precariously balanced into debt. Meanwhile, Mother's condition was worsening.

All seemed bad and growing worse when a surprise came in the form of the Showman calling upon my father at the shop— he was opening a second, even more astounding museum and was in need of all the oddities he could get his hands on. Father had continued to purchase curiosities from his vendors after the previous museum's destruction, and at a steep discount—after all, he shrewdly reasoned to them, what price could he get for them now that the famous museum had been destroyed? The

---

[28] If Zara's father, as she claims earlier, was a physician in his homeland, why would he call one to care for his own wife? And if his previous profession was a fabrication, was it Zara's? A story told to her by her mother? Or could her father also have had a bit of the humbug in him?

Showman now offered to purchase the entire collection, Father had only to name his price. Expecting to haggle, Father doubled the price he wanted.

"Sold!" the Showman declared.

I now spied a way out of being my mother's nursemaid and ending our cycle of near poverty. I would return to work at the new museum! But Father was not so keen on my plan. Who would care for Mother when I was away at work? I reasoned that my wages at the museum could pay for a caretaker while I was away. Father no more liked the idea of a stranger caring for Mother than he believed I could make enough money to both cover the cost of her care and make up for lost income, and thought—with maddeningly circular logic—that even if I could, it was a waste of money to spend it on care when I could be her nurse at no cost. Looking back, I can see the worry it caused him to have his beloved wife looked after by a stranger when he was unable to be home with her himself, but, being a teenager,[29] I simply saw him as a stubborn old goat.

Shortly after the museum opened, I took matters into my own hands. One afternoon, without Father's knowledge, I hired a nurse to watch Mother for a few hours and went to the museum myself. I was welcomed with open arms by the same manager who had helped me to pull the ruse on the British Prince. He gave me a tour of the new museum, which boasted an even grander collection that the previous one. He took me to see my old friends in their new residences and there was much embracing and teasing over how I had grown into a woman since we had last met.[30]

---

[29] Sarah Selinsky would have been about twenty-one by this time.

[30] Between the fire and the opening of Putnam's new museum, eight months passed.

And then, at last, the Showman was there, beaming as broadly as ever, proud of his new establishment and by all appearances completely sanguine over the loss of his previous one. He greeted me as his own daughter and asked what brought me to see him. When I asked if I might return to his employ, his face fell.

"I'm afraid we've staffed up on ticket girls, dressers, and housemaids," he said. "Our roster of employees has been filled. All except…"

His eyes fell upon my hair. Even pulled tightly back as it was, ripples betrayed the unruly curls I had always struggled to control. My hair was thick and black, like my mother's, and stood in contrast to the pale gray eyes I had also inherited from her.

"Our Moss-Haired Girl is currently at large," he continued. "Have you ever considered a career in show business?"

My father was none too keen on the idea, particularly after learning how I had conspired to get away to meet with the Showman, but once I told him how much the job would pay (he could hire a clerk for the shop to take his place and a nursemaid if he so desired, and there would be money to spare!), he saw there was no other decision to be made. The very next day, I packed my few possessions and moved into the museum.

A tailor was brought in to create a costume for me, a beautiful thing of midnight blue and violet silk with gold-braid trim and a scandalously low neckline. The skirt would be quite abbreviated, reaching to just above the knee, with pink satin bloomers peeking out just below. The Showman was consulted over the matter of a name, and after some discussion, I was re-christened Zara Zalinzi. There was only one missing piece that remained of my transformation—my hair.

First, it would have to be cut. Anticipating the tears of an ordinary girl, the woman who wielded the scissors was apologetic and tender, but I was not sorry to see it go. I had been wrestling with it all my life, and as far as I was concerned, it would be a relief if there were less of it. As I watched it fall to the floor, I could feel myself grow lighter.

The hairdresser was astonished at the way it sprang up into a dense cloud of coils of its own accord as she snipped away. I will admit to some dismay at the sight of it in the mirror—I had always hated the way it looked when untamed—but it was necessary to complete the process. I next reclined, my head in a tub of smelly stale beer. At last, the hairdresser checked her watch and allowed me to sit up. When my hair had dried she went at it a bit with a comb, admitting that she really didn't have much work to do. With her help, I slipped into my full costume for the first time and examined myself in a full-length mirror. I was taken aback by what I saw, a regal and mysterious woman now stood where there had been a rather ridiculous and silly little girl.[31]

The dresser called for the Showman. Upon seeing me in costume for the first time, his face lit up in a grin and he asked me to execute a full turn. I did so slowly and confidently, feeling that the costume had transformed me through some sort of alchemy into the character I was going to play. The Showman laughed and declared the metamorphosis an unqualified success.

---

[31] My sister, who ironed her hair throughout high school to make it look "normal," joined the hippie movement in college. One of her early acts of social protest was to stop setting her hair, cut it short, and pick it into an Afro. Rereading Zara's account of her transformation, I was reminded of how Leah had described similar feelings when talking about her own hair before and after she let it be what it was naturally. While trying to keep it under control, she saw the kinkiness as ugly and somehow exposing something hidden that she was ashamed of, but with her hair in its natural state, she felt powerful and beautiful.

When I emerged from my room, all my dear friends were waiting in the hall to see what I had become. I stepped forward, a hand on one hip, and raised my chin high to the sound of their applause. I have never treasured the sound so much before an audience of strangers as I did before my friends that day. I even saw the lips of the ever-glowering Strong Man turn up in a smile, the sight of which recalled to me the previously forgotten feeling of receiving the kiss of the British Prince on the back of my hand.

At my first performance, my part was simply to stand while the Showman spoke. He explained to a rapt audience that I was a princess from Circassia, a region in the Caucasus Mountains where the purest examples of the white race could be found.[32]

The Showman told the crowd that I had recently been purchased by his agent, who had been in disguise as a Turkish Prince at a slave auction, and had outbid all the lustful Turks who had come to purchase prizes for their harems. In addition to being the embodiment of the ideal of feminine beauty, I was also a great intellect, and though I could speak eight languages that they knew of, English was not yet one of them, so it was requested that

---

[32] This was the sideshow barker's standard spiel about the Circassian Beauty. In point of fact, there are a Circassian people, known to each other as the Adyghe, and for centuries, the women of the Adyghe have indeed been prized for their beauty and gentility. This fact had made it to the U.S. by at least the early 18th century, when the images of Circassian women could be found on beauty products. The theory that the Circassians possessed a higher racial purity had been posited in the early 19th century by the same misguided scientist who had coined the term "Caucasian" to refer to the white race, naming it after the region where he believed the purest examples of the race could be found. In 1862, after years of conflict, the Circassians were displaced from their home in the Russian Conquest of the Caucasus Mountains, an event that was big news all over the world. H. R. Putnam saw an opportunity

members of the audience refrain from addressing me directly. In order to further titillate, it was revealed in hushed tones that I had been betrothed to a Circassian Prince but was stolen away in the night by the Turks on the eve of my wedding, and since I had just come to market when I was rescued, I was, in all likelihood, still a maiden. I could feel the crowd stirring at the lurid tale and, allowing my eyes to sweep across them, saw blushes paint the cheeks of young ladies and men alike while older gentlemen coughed into their handkerchiefs and their wives tut-tutted. I was an instant sensation.

Another new act had joined the troupe, a striking man with a shock of auburn hair who both sang under the title of Llew Arvon, the Lion of Carnarvon, and performed feats of ventriloquism as Professor Hughs. On the night of my first performance, he was onstage after me, and I could feel him watching me from the wings. Though he was a dignified man, I could sense his interest was more than intellectual, and my suspicions were confirmed that very evening when he introduced himself and invited me to take supper with him in his room. He was quite charming about it and his speaking voice was as mellifluous as his singing, and I confess to feeling somewhat torn in declining his invitation as entirely too forward. He seemed almost pleased by my refusal and took it as encouragement. Thereafter, he courted me in a gentle-manly and persistent manner. Eventually the Showman noticed a

---

for the museum and, so the story goes, sent an agent to purchase a Circassian girl at a Turkish auction. When the agent returned empty-handed, Putnam found a curly-haired local girl who was willing to subject herself to a beer shampoo and a skimpy "Turkish" costume, and put her on display. The Circassian Beauty was a smash hit and became a mainstay in sideshows all over the country for the next thirty years.

spark between us and we were billed as a newly married couple, though little more had passed between us than a bit of flirting. In our new act, the Lion was the distinguished Englishman[33] who had taken on the task of teaching me the language which I might more easily navigate my way back home to my Prince, but in so doing, had fallen hopelessly in love with me. Fortunately for him, I had done the same, and though he had to occasionally weather my stormy moods as I recalled the glory of my former home, the Prince I had left behind, and the king and queen who surely mourned the absence of their dear daughter, he was able to cheer me with his beautiful singing or, when that failed, making it appear that the family cat were speaking or his own voice was emanating from inside the piano. I now spoke on stage, and I did so in the Professor's accent. After all, it was he who had taught me English. I know not whether the Showman was acting as Cupid or merely spied an opportunity for an unusual story to tell before the public, but it had the effect of turning a tall tale into a truth. The Lion and I were soon married.[34]

At this time the Circassian Beauty that I had replaced had finally turned up.[35]

At first I feared I may have just been a temporary replacement, but the Showman declared there was room for two Moss-Haired

---

[33] Everything about the names that the Professor performed under indicated he was Welsh. If you've ever mistakenly called a Welshman English to his face, you'll know the cardinal sin that Putnam was committing in telling this particular whopper.

[34] A record exists for the 1865 New York marriage of a Sarah Selitsky and an R. L. Hughes, occupation: singer.

[35] Imza Adzel began reappearing in bills for the museum at about the same time that Zara and Hughs became a double bill.

Girls. Now, when the Lion was performing at other engagements across town, we two Circassian Girls would appear as sisters reunited far from home by the Showman, who continued to send his agent in search of innocents, bound for the harem, to rescue. Off the stage, we became very close; she still recalled how I had helped prepare her for the show just a few years before. Though she was very popular, she was older than I, and I oft times sensed she was reminded of her increasing age by my youth. I regularly assured her that she remained one of the most enduring beauties I had ever seen, a statement that seemed to comfort her.[36]

One night I chanced upon my husband half-hidden in a dark corner of the museum, where he was talking low to a woman in a manner that I found most troubling. Imagine my shock when the woman stepped into the light and I saw that it was my dear friend, the Circassian Girl! I hid behind a heavy curtain as she passed, then waited until I was alone with the Lion to ask about what I had witnessed. He assured me that he had merely been consoling her over a personal matter and I had nothing to fear, and he was so tender towards me that I felt silly for asking. But I saw them together again on a few occasions after that, and could not quite shake the shameful suspicion that plagued me. Soon it became known among the residents that he had developed a frequent habit of entering and exiting her quarters. It had also come to my attention that he was rather too fond of drink, something I tried to keep from the Showman, who was a fervent Temperance man.[37]

But soon I had another concern. My father sent word that

---

[36] Here we see either Zara's vanity or her need to under-report her true age showing through. In a photo that survives of Imza Adzel and Zara together, it's impossible to tell who is older.

[37] Putnam was a well-known tee-totaller.

Mother had taken a turn for the worse and I had better come home if I was ever to see her again. I did so with haste.

The difference in her appearance in the time I had been away was sobering. Her thick, dark hair was thinned and wispy and what remained was almost entirely gray. She had lost so much weight that her skin draped hollow over her cheekbones, and she seemed to have shrunk in her bed. My father, too, had aged years in those few months while watching her decline. I sent word that I wouldn't be returning to the museum for a time.

Father sent the nursemaid home and we cared for Mother together until her passing one beautiful spring morning. Though the gloom of that day was heavy, we were gladdened to see the smile on her face as she passed. Father wanted her to be buried with the brooch he had given her upon their engagement, an inexpensive thing she had always cherished over more valuable pieces of jewellery. I set to work looking for it, and after an extensive search, found it in a box on her vanity. Beneath the brooch, there was a photo of a handsome and distinguished older couple in elaborate formal dress. On the reverse was signed in beautiful script, "Love, Mother." This was the photo Mother looked at every day that I had never seen, the photo of the grandparents I had never met.[38]

It was only days after Mother's funeral that I learned I was not sick from merely grief. I returned to the museum to tell the Lion I was carrying his child and that, furthermore, I was fully aware of his dalliance. He fell to his knees, clasping me to him while weeping with joy and contrition, promising his days of roving and drunkenness were over. I could smell the bourbon on his breath

---

[38] This inscription is the same as the one on the photo given to my wife by Sarah M., though Zara's description is in sharp contrast to its appearance.

as he wept into my skirts, but I forgave him anyhow. I wanted so much for life to be perfect that I believed I could will it to be if I were strong enough.

As for the Showman, naturally he was overjoyed by the baby's impending arrival—he adored the prospect of expanding our act as much as he adored me and wished for my happiness.

.

The penmanship of the signer would be better described as child-like than "beautiful script." The couple pictured is not in fancy dress, but wearing patched and threadbare rags. If Sarah M.'s picture is the photo of Zara's grandparents, Zara wasn't lying when she described them as handsome and distinguished—despite the rags they wear, and the deep lines etched by toil and cruelty into their gaunt faces, their dignity shines through.

The most frustratingly elusive questions in my research surround just what Zara knew, when she knew it, and how she felt about it. Was this the first moment Zara knew she was the grandchild of slaves? Did she feel anger at having had the truth hidden from her? Sudden understanding? Shame? Pride? Did she confront her father with questions? Or did she pin the brooch to the collar of the shirt on her mother's cooling body, tuck the photo away, and turn her attention back to practical matters and her grieving father? Had she already known and so the photo held no deeper surprises than whether she took after her mother's side or her father's?

Unfortunately, she does not linger here.

CHAPTER FOUR

A BABY PRODIGY IS BORN—A TIME OF GREAT SUCCESS—

COMPETITION IN THE RANKS—BAD HABITS RETURN—AN

UNLIKELY RESCUE—FIRE AGAIN AND ANOTHER RESCUE—

AN UNCERTAIN FUTURE—ORPHANED AND ALONE

T he prospect of fatherhood turned the Lion into a model husband. Many times I felt the jealous glare of the other Circassian Girl, no longer my dear friend, which confirmed the Lion had returned his full attention to his wife. My costume was altered to encompass my expanding waistline until propriety deemed it necessary to step down from the stage for a time. It was explained to the audience that I was in a delicate state and the Lion performed alone, demonstrating the ways he would entertain his impending issue with ventriloquism, and refusing the comically sour-faced advances of another Circassian Beauty intent on stealing his heart while his true love was indisposed.

When the child was born,[39] the Lion was over the moon to learn it was a boy. The Showman wasted no time in having the

---

[39] And with it, yet another mystery. An exhaustive search of variants on the names of both parents has turned up no birth record for this child. Because of this lack of information, the possibility cannot be ruled out that this pairing never resulted in children and the child who appeared in the act was a local baby for hire. Putnam was not above the practice of hiring babies and often employed it when exhibiting his midgets and their "children." Zara claims to have had two children over the course of her life (there is no birth record for a second, either) and, since she has descendants, there must be some truth to this. It is possible that she was indeed raising the child as her own, but it was not hers biologically. If it was her own, extrapolating the approximate

baby's first tiny suit made, and soon I was back on stage with the babe in my arms, the Showman declaring before an audience that upon being swatted at his birth, the Baby Beethoven wailed the first two measures of the Fifth Symphony. A miniature piano was made for him, and by the time he could stand he could play "Mary Had a Little Lamb" to the accompaniment of his father, whose flourishes on the violin coupled with my singing in the Lion's tutored accent gave the illusion of a more skilled performance than it was. Quickly, the popularity of our act overtook that of the previous reigning billed couple, the Bearded Lady and the Strong Man. I felt no animosity toward the former, and even wished to be friends, but she was so spiteful I almost took pleasure in unseating her. Fond of smoking cigars, on more than one occasion she held the burning butt so close to my hair that it could have been singed, and she once spilled wine on my gown just before a performance, shamming her apology so outrageously that even the Strong Man was seen to roll his eye. A silken sash was found to cover up the stain, I went on stage as scheduled, and the cost of the repair to my costume came out of her pay. All of this only seemed to inflame her hatred of me.

Other dangers lurked. During one performance by the Moss-Haired Girl, the Professor, and the Baby Beethoven, the Showman opened up the floor to questions. A pretty young girl with smooth yellow hair in the crowd coyly asked if my husband had always been so taken by black curls. Because the Showman always encouraged us to flatter the crowd, the Lion replied that there was a time before he had laid eyes on my exotic beauty, in fact, where he had imagined that he preferred

---

birthdate from Baby Beethoven's first appearance in the act suggests that the baby predates the marriage by at least a year. If he was the issue of Zara and the Lion, she was not so chaste through their courtship as she claims.

light-haired girls. She blushed and giggled, and I thought no more of it until later that night, when I returned from the parlour to spy her in the residents' wing, slipping from my husband's room. Her inebriation was apparent from the way she giggled and stumbled as she snuck to the stairs. My heart sank—I could only assume my husband was within his quarters in a similar state. That he had allowed someone from the outside into the sanctum we shared with our fellow performers was perhaps more unforgivable than what he had done with her inside his room—he would have been cast out had anyone else but me discovered her. Now fearing our brittle union might shatter if I were to confront him, I kept silent, but this event was soon followed by many other dalliances.

One night, I finally felt I had had enough. I gathered my courage and confronted him. The drink, which could either make him a lion or a lamb, had, unfortunately for me, turned him into a beast on that occasion. A cold gleam in his eye, he confessed to the misdeeds in question, then many others, then declared his intention to leave his habits unchanged. When I told him that I would be seeking a divorce and he would not be allowed to see our child, he flew into a rage and struck me a blow. I fell to the floor, cowering beneath the Lion's upraised hand, certain I was about to meet my end.

There came a knock at the door. Once I had collected myself, the Lion opened the door to find the Strong Man looming before him. He looked at my husband, then to me. Still trembling, I put on a false smile.

"I do apologize!" I said brightly. "It is rather late for one of our lively debates. I should get to my room. Goodnight, Husband."

The Strong Man watched as I retired to my room, one brooding eye on the Lion's door. Before I shut my own, I looked back to him, feeling a need to say something, but not knowing quite what. His brooding expression softened in response to my beseeching look, and it seemed that words were not necessary. With that, I closed the door.

In the morning I stayed in my quarters with the baby, fretting over facing my husband. When I finally emerged, I saw that I needn't have worried, for he was uninterested in speaking to me. To my dismay and the Bearded Woman's delight, the Lion thenceforth took up dalliances as his primary hobby, parading them before me whenever he could. On stage we continued to be the picture of domestic bliss, although, perhaps sensing our disconnect, the Showman began inserting more flourishes in our spiel about the Circassian Girl's mournful soul and the Lion's selfish roar casting a shadow over the happy family.

The Showman's tale predicted the future once more when the baby proved to be a prodigy gifted at music who amazed the crowd more and more with each performance. The child, at least, was my great joy, and so I took to spending spare hours alone with my son in our room. Though I still had dear friends at the museum, I could not bear to speak with them, knowing all could see my husband turning his back on our wedding vows. I considered leaving the museum, but how would I raise my child without my weekly pay? What would happen if I tried to leave? Would the Lion demand to have his child in his custody? How would I ever find another place that would feel as much like home? I was paralyzed with indecision, so I continued to play at my role onstage while hiding from all in my room offstage.

One night I was awakened by the sound of glass shattering and found the room was thick with smoke. Coughing, I stumbled to the pitcher to wet a cloth and place it over the baby's mouth. I felt my way to the door, but the brass handle was too hot to touch. I looked out the window to see the light from the flames illuminate the street six storeys below. The other museum residents were wrapped in blankets, watching their home burn down before them once again.[40]

I saw my dear Giantess raise her hand in a panic to point to my stricken face in the window, and a ripple of fear ran through the dear motley group of them. The Strong Man's eyes met mine. Trapped, I clutched the weeping baby to my bosom and sank out of the thick of the smoke to the floor, praying for rescue as my lungs burned and the room began to spin. How long I sat there, willing myself to stay awake, I do not know, but at last a peace fell over me. I was ready to meet my fate.

Suddenly, the door burst from its hinges. There, silhouetted in flame, stood the Strong Man. He strode into the room, scooped me up in his massive arms with ease, baby and all, and carried us to safety outside. It was only when he had gently lowered us to the ground that I saw the toll the act had taken on him, for he lost consciousness himself. The Bearded Lady rushed to his side in fear, and I suddenly understood the root of her unpleasant temperament—the poor ornery creature was in love with him.

Our beloved museum home destroyed and our dejected Showman in retreat, we show folk scattered to find new homes.

I returned to my father's lonely apartment. The Lion and I now estranged,[41] I was safe to take on the child's care alone without fear of losing him. Father had grown thin and anxious and it

---

[40] Putnam's second museum was also destroyed by fire a mere three years following its grand opening. This time he did not race to rebuild.

[41] No explanation has been found for the Lion's sudden disinterest in the custody of his child. One has to wonder if he had ever even met his in-laws. This could be further evidence in support of the idea that the baby was for hire, but it could also indicate that Zara was reluctant to share her true origins with Hughs or, if she did, that he did not react favourably.

seemed the baby was the only thing in life to bring a smile to his face. Much like us, the tiny piano had survived with only a little scorching to betray its near-destruction, and evenings after supper, Father would play his instruments while the baby accompanied him and I sang along. Though Father's shop was profitable and I had saved enough to keep us comfortable for some time, he worried over every cent. He was so frail that I fell to constantly worrying myself every day when he left to keep the shop, then nearly weeping with relief to see him come home. I determined to live every moment with him in as jolly a manner as I could, so to raise his spirits I often spun tales of my time at the museum, all the while wondering if it had come to an end. Would I ever stand before a crowd as a beautiful foreign Princess in peril? Would I ever meet my dear friends again? Would the chance to properly thank the Strong Man for saving my life ever come? At times I even wished to see the Bearded Lady once more.

Father delighted in the stories I told and laughed to hear the tales the Showman made up about me as the Circassian Girl. He regretted that he had never seen me perform and promised that, should I return to that vocation, he would not miss it for the world.[42]

But, alas, it was never to be. Father dropped dead of an apoplexy one day in the shop, and I found myself an orphan raising a child alone.[43]

---

[42] This seems extremely progressive for a father in the late 19th century, given the lurid nature of the Circassian Beauty's spiel and the revealing (by the day's standards) costumes they wore. Perhaps Zara wasn't completely forthcoming with her father on the true nature of her role?

[43] A death record for a Sol Salinsky [sic], born in Russia, exists in the New York City vital records collection. It lists his death by heart attack at age fifty-eight on October 11, 1869.

CHAPTER FIVE

THE SHOW GOES ON—A JOYOUS REUNION—RECON-
CILIATION—A ROYAL REUNION—THE LADY LASHES
OUT—CONFESSIONS OF LOVE—ON THIN ICE

Many of Father's friends and business acquaintances paid their respects upon his death, and I was moved to see the number of people who had admired and adored him. But the person I was most glad to see was the Showman, who seemed genuinely aggrieved by Father's passing. He confessed that his visit was twofold: to bring his condolences and to invite me to join a tour he was organizing for Great Britain.[44]

I left Father's clerk in charge of the shop after hiring a former museum worker to assist him, and packed my trunk. Soon I was travelling first class on a steamer bound for England, reunited with many of my dear friends. The Giantess was there, along with the Giant, whom the Showman was billing as her mate (special quarters had been modified for their comfort).[45]

The Skeleton Man had brought his wife and the three strapping boys he had sired whom he was so proud of. My dear

---

[44] Putnam took his most popular performers on a successful tour of the U.K. in the winter of 1869-70.

[45] Mabel Birch and General Magnus, though lifelong friends, were never a couple. It was not for lack of trying on his part, however. According to his autobiography, he proposed to her on a weekly basis right up to her death, and though he lived thirty years more, he never fell in love again.

armless friend greeted me with kisses in lieu of an embrace, and of course there was the Showman's star attraction, his beloved midget. I smiled so with happiness at the sight of the Bearded Lady that she was momentarily disarmed. The Lion was also there, and took a moment alone with me to declare that he had been a beast, would understand if I refused to resume our former act as a family, and would make the matter clear himself to the Showman if I so desired. Feeling this was the wisest course of action I requested that he do so, and he agreed to the terms with no sign of animosity.

At first sight of the Strong Man, I was at a loss. I found myself more thrilled to see him now than I had ever been at the sight of the Lion. I had not laid eyes on him since he had rescued the baby and myself from the flames, and, despite the length of our acquaintance, words had never passed between us. But once again, as our eyes met, it seemed we didn't need them.

The voyage was a merry one, full of remembrances and news of other performers who were not on the tour. The joy of being once again in the bosom of friendship was almost unbearable. Even the Lion was on his best behaviour—the prettiest of passengers seemed enthralled by his thick auburn hair and fine dress but not a single one turned his eye. At first I forbade him to see the baby, but there was such a pain in the Lion's eye when someone else asked after the child or I took him for a walk on the deck within the Lion's view that I soon relented. The Lion was a perfect gentleman to me and made no advances. By voyage's end, we were almost as good as a family again and I had reversed my position on our act, but I would require that we once again have separate lodging for our travels. The Lion agreed that was for the best.

It was a grand tour. Between engagements it was easy for me to slip out unnoticed—all I had to do was twist my hair under a hat and don a modest outfit—and so I saw much of the country on foot. Of our many stops, one of the most memorable was the visit to the palace where I was reunited with the very man whose entrance to the Showman's museum I had barred and I had astonished by holding out my hand in demand for a ticket. Once the Showman had provided his introduction to our exotic musical family and we had performed *God Save the Queen* in perfect harmony, he and the Princess applauded and he stepped forth. Like the regal Princess of the mountains I was, I imperiously held out my hand, and he bent to kiss the back of it, pausing for a moment as he looked into my eyes with a half-remembered recognition, then shook it off. The royal visit was a smashing success, and the raves of the royals ensured our success for the remainder of the tour. But there was one among us who could not seem to enjoy it. The Bearded Lady had been told by the Prince, who had intended it a compliment, that her facial growth was heartier than his own, and enviously so. Having felt her whiskers a plague ever since they appeared, this was another stab to her hidden tender heart.

One night, I awoke to see her looming over my bed in the darkness, a gleaming pair of sharpened scissors in her hand. I heard the snip and felt my own hair fall upon my cheek. Screaming, I pushed her from me.

"Come sister," she entreated me. "I will cut yours, then you will cut mine."

I assured her I would do no such thing, nor should she, for our respective hairs were our source of livelihood. She began to weep and swore she cared not; she could not live with it any longer. Holding the scissors out, she implored me to take them and free her of her whiskers. The Bearded Lady's eyes then took on a frightening gleam. She charged at me, the scissors held out like a knife. I managed to catch her by the wrist as she fell upon me, and we tumbled to the floor, struggling, as I cried out for help. What seemed like an eternity passed, during which the baby screamed from where he cowered in a corner. I was nicked by the blade more than once before I finally heard the frantic sounds of voices calling out with concern and pounding on the door, all in vain, for the Bearded Lady had locked it from the inside.

The door burst open at last. In came the Strong Man, who set to work prying the wild woman from me. When the Bearded Lady recognized my defender, she became even more enraged and turned her wrath upon him. Screams emanated from her that raised goose-pimples all over my skin, the screams of an animal. It took four men to subdue her and the Strong Man was cut in the fray by the flashing scissors. In time, orderlies arrived from a local asylum to take her away.[46]

My wounds, which were thankfully superficial and would not show when I was in costume, were dressed, as were those of the

---

[46] The breakdown that terminated Madame Anya's stint on Putnam's tour of Great Britain (and seemingly her career as a performer) is documented, though not in detail. Papers reported a variety of speculative stories as to what happened that night—some said she had gone after her own child, some said she had tried to kill herself over an unresponsive lover, and one even put forth the possibility that she was really a man and had finally cracked over living a lie. Interestingly, all of the reports agreed on one thing— Anya had incurred some frightening wounds herself, and witnesses in the crowd that had gathered outside the hotel were doubtful she would survive. It sounds like either Zara or Ivan fought back more fiercely than Zara relates here.

Madame Anya disappears from the records for a long time before she shows up in the 1920 U.S. census, curiously enough, married to a railroad engineer in Ohio. It is not known what became of her child, the side effect of whose birth was also the birth of her sideshow career.

Strong Man, which required more attention, and we found ourselves alone in my room. The baby had cried himself to sleep in my arms. I looked to my knight in shining armour, who had now saved my life three times over, and could no longer be silent.

"Thank you," I said, simply.

He smiled and the gloom lifted from his gaze. "De nada," he replied.

The Siberian strong man was Spanish![47]

We laughed a moment, then the mood turned serious once more. He took my hand in his and solemnly declared his love. My father had taught me enough Spanish that, between what I knew of his tongue and he knew of English, we had no trouble understanding one another. Tears spilling from my eyes, I returned his declaration in kind, but remembered to him my wedding vows. He nodded, gently releasing my hand. Before withdrawing from the room, he tenderly caressed the baby's head and assured me that his heart had been true since I was a ticket girl at the Showman's first museum, and that it would always be so. As the door closed behind him, I wept softly, understanding at last that I felt the same.

In the morning it was discovered that the Lion, having stepped out for a walk in the night air and never returned to his room, had missed the melodrama of the previous evening. I feared he might have been up to his old tricks again, but he was still absent when the curtain rose for our next engagement, and we all began

---

[47] Zara is the only source for Ivan the Great's supposed true nationality. Because she never reveals his given name, and he is not referred to anywhere in print or memory as anything other than Ivan the Great (with the exception of his later incarnation as Prince Zoltan), his nationality, as well as his identity, remains a mystery.

to worry. By the second missed performance, the Showman had notified the police that he was missing.

He turned up again just in time for the next performance, drunk, dirty, and with a terrible black eye, held up by the arm of a girl of questionable repute.[48]

The Showman nearly fired him on the spot, but, fearing for the happiness of our child, who adored his father, I implored him to give the Lion a chance to shape up. Reluctantly, he allowed it, but made it clear that there could be no more incidents.[49]

It was just as clear to me, at last, that the Lion would never be the husband I desired. Still, I honoured our vows and was chaste in my interactions with the Strong Man.

---

[48] Write-ups in local British papers on three sequential performances of the tour mention Hughs's absence due to "another engagement," suggesting he had been on the bill but had not performed. If Zara's account is true and he had been reported missing and found to just be on a bender, it's a testament to Putnam's relationship with the press that the incident never appeared in print.

[49] It appears that Hughs was present and accounted for for the remainder of the tour, but the Showman had no further plans when it ended, so the performers were once again cast adrift.

CHAPTER SIX

BACK AT HOME—A LETTER RECEIVED LATE—UNDER

THE BIG TOP—A DOUBLE TRAGEDY —AN

EXTRAORDINARY VISIT

Back in the States, the Lion was as contrite as ever. We stayed in Father's apartment with the baby for a time, considering what to do next. The Lion had a notion to tour the dime museums, but that seemed to me a step down from the grand adventures we had been having both in scale and dignity. We hemmed and hawed over it as we chipped away at our earnings from the tour. A rather large pile of letters had accumulated in my absence, so I took to the task of sorting and answering this correspondence. In the process I made a most exciting find—a letter addressed to my mother in the same beautiful script that had inscribed her precious photo!

From the date inside the envelope, it seemed to have taken some time to reach us, the delay explained by the fact that the missive was addressed to Mother's name but without address. Despite the years, I thought I could smell a hint of fine perfume on the delicate paper. With trembling hands, I carefully opened the letter and read the contents. The letter was from my grandmother, who reported that Grandfather had passed away and, since it was safe, Mother could now come home to visit. She spoke of how sorry she was that so many years had come between them and that she wished they could be together once more before she followed Grandfather to the grave. The tears flowed as I realized that my mother had still been alive when the letter was written, but by the time it found its way to us, Grandmother had outlived her.[50]

As I carefully tucked the letter back into its envelope, I imagined how it would have consoled my mother to know she was welcome in her comfortable childhood home as she mourned the death of my brother in this cramped apartment. The thought was too much to bear. Soon the baby was at my side, patting my cheek with his small hand.

"Don't cry, Mommy," said my little boy, "don't cry. We will go to the circus again." I lifted him up, kissing him and laughing through my tears.

"Yes, my little darling, that we will!"

I soon had the opportunity to make good on my promise when word came that the Showman was preparing a travelling show to tour America. It was to be the biggest show yet staged and would require the help of all show folk he had ever had the pleasure to work with. The Lion and I at last agreed on something, that there was no question in the matter—we were going.

---

[50] This letter still exists and was also in Sarah M.'s possession. Wilma, possessor of the "auntie" photo, also has a very similar letter addressed to Gaby and received by Sarah Selinsky's oldest sister, suggesting copies might have gone out to all of Gaby's siblings in the hopes that one of them might have been able to pass it on to her. Again, between the perfume and the penmanship, Zara lays the fantasy on thick. In actuality, the same child-like handwriting that appears on the backs of the photos has further degraded, likely due to the author's advanced age. The summation of the contents is more or less accurate, but the language is much less eloquent, though considerably more poignant.

There are two possible interpretations to the remark that it was "safe" to return home. The first, and presumably the one Zara intends us to believe, is that it was her father's banishment that kept Gaby away. The more likely interpretation is borne out by the date of the letter, July 21st, 1865, after the Civil War had ended and slaves in the south were free.

Once again we were reunited with old friends. I was gladdened to see my Strong Man again, but it was bittersweet to realize my love for him had only grown. With the Bearded Lady gone, he was no longer paired with a mate when he performed. He was now presented as a man who had grown wild in Siberian exile, dressed in ragged furs with tangled hair, a lone beast who could only be tamed by the love he left behind. To erase any doubt of his wildness, he was now growling in response to questions from the crowd.

I was, as ever, the Circassian Princess stolen from the arms of her soon-to-be husband and waylaid by an Englishman who could not resist the Oriental charms of my perfect Caucasian beauty.[51]

Since the Showman felt that Mozart was experiencing more popularity, our son was now dressed in a frock coat and powdered wig and billed as Little Wolfgang, born wailing the first two measures of *Eine kleine Nachtmusik*. Together we were a family that breathed music and lived with passionate abandon. Except, of

---

[51] By now it is safe to assume she knew of her mother's origins. If only some record survived on how she felt about being held up as the perfect white woman in her act! Did it make her furious that her job was to glorify the ideal of white beauty trumping all? Or did she laugh behind the backs of gullible audiences who would accept without question that a seemingly white girl with an Afro was an exemplification of the purity of the white race?

Photos of her contemporaries show that some Circassian Beauties were very likely of mixed race. It was a popular act and performers travelled around frequently. The odds are good that she met other mixed-race Circassian performers in her nearly twenty years of show business. Was there an acknowledgement of their origins in their own circles, unspoken or otherwise? Or was it yet another fact that was unimportant in the self-made family of the sideshow, where identities were (and still are) remade and accepted without question?

course, for those times I reflected back on the family I had lost and the man I had left behind, and I became melancholy and inconsolable while the Lion's jealousy cast a shadow over us all.

Performing with old friends again was a balm to my spirit. Though the love I had had for the Lion had been lost, we were on civil, even friendly terms. And the show was a marvel. It was the most enormous spectacle anyone had ever seen, and, despite its size, somehow it closed in one town, then opened up again in another the very next day. It seemed all was as well as it had ever been. But one night, as I drifted to sleep, lulled by the music of the tracks as we steamed to our next destination, one of the cars slipped the track. I awoke to the terrible sounds of screeching metal, screaming passengers, and panicked animals as more than half of the train was derailed. Though there were more than sixty cars, there were only two deaths—my husband and my beloved baby boy.[52]

---

[52] This accident is well documented. Though, as with the two museum fires, there were a tragic number of animal casualties, there were no reports of human deaths. However, it is a fact that Hughs and Little Wolfgang disappear from billing around this time—a little before the accident, in fact, somewhere in Ohio. Where did they go? On a hunch, I began searching Ohio records for Richard Hughs after his disappearance from the travelling show. Due to the large influx of Welsh immigrants to the state, not to mention the long-standing patronymic naming system that resulted in the top ten Welsh surnames being held by 90 percent of the Welsh population, I had my work cut out for me. At last I found a good suspect—a Richard Hughes, music teacher, who was listed in the 1880 U.S. Census for Ohio with this wife and three children. As I zeroed in on this family I found more clues. His daughter listed him in her marriage record as "Professor Hughes." This might not be a smoking gun—after all, a music teacher could easily be a professor—but then I came across a self-published history of the small town this professor lived in. In it, this Professor Hughes was described as a former travelling performer

The grief was unbearable. I continued to perform, of course, but could not find my previous enjoyment in the role-playing. My Strong Man could not bear to see me so devastated, but there was naught he could do to ease my sorrows. A less gentlemanly fellow might have taken advantage of my vulnerable state, but he kept his distance, promising that he would be there for me when I felt ready for his comfort.

Frequently, I took out the letter from my grandmother and the photo that Mother had held so dear. I had never known the love of a grandmother and I yearned for it so.

One day, at the same moment I was gazing at her beautiful handwriting, I realized that we were heading for the very town the letter had been sent from! I went to see the Showman to beg for the day off. He granted it with his blessing.

Not knowing where to find her, I went into the post office to inquire after the address. It was quite a way from the centre of town, so I hired a carriage, my heart in my throat the whole drive, wondering if she would be happy to see me. Mother never gave any indication that she was keeping up with anyone in the family

---

with a beautiful singing voice and a skill for entertaining the children by making it sound as if his voice was coming from the inside of the piano he played. He died in 1893 (coincidentally, the same year Putnam was laid to rest) of unknown causes. On one of my trips to Ohio I visited the cemetery outside this Richard Hughes's small town. There, he was, beside his wife Mary. His gravestone named him as Richard L. Hughes, "LLEW ARFON." If this was Zara's husband, and it seems it must have been, it looks like he fled in the night with their son, either in pursuit of this Mary or in search of a new life, and Zara covered up the truth with a story about their deaths. But where is the child, then? A possible suspect turns up in an orphan's home not long after the Lion disappears, perhaps surrendered by Hughs, then disappears again. But we may not have seen the last of him ...

while she was alive. Would Grandmother even know she had a granddaughter?

At last the carriage stopped before the grandest plantation house I had ever seen. A maid greeted me at the door.[53]

I introduced myself, holding out the photo then turning it over to show the inscription, just in case they thought I was an impostor bent on stealing her wealth. I was asked to wait outside while the photo was taken inside. It seemed to take an eternity, and after a time I began to worry I would never see the photo again. The door finally opened and the maid beckoned me to enter, then led me to a grand library.

In it, a tiny shrunken woman dressed in fine old-fashioned silk and lace sat in a wheelchair. She looked so much like Mother would have if she had not died so young that I was shaken for a moment. She squinted, nearly blind, when I entered the room.

"So you are Gabrella's daughter?" she said. "Come closer, dear child, where I can see you."

I knelt beside her, the tears welling in my eyes. She touched my face, beaming. "Where is your mother, dear?"

The tears spilled over as I told her what had become of Mother, Father, brother, husband, and son. I laid my head upon her knee, where she petted it then sang a pretty song until the tears finally

---

[53] According to Sarah M., the actual house was a shotgun shack and, since Gaby's mother Sarah was its sole occupant in the 1870 census just two years before, she was most likely the only person in it when Zara came to call. What was it like the first time Zara laid eyes on the house her mother grew up in? Was it what she expected or was she taken aback? Did it change her feelings about her mother or herself? I made an attempt to find this house, one of a small cluster of dwellings still noted on survey maps as late as the 1960s, but the area was abandoned, deemed an eyesore, and razed decades ago. A Piggly Wiggly parking lot now covers the approximate spot.

stopped. To my great surprise, I felt more at peace than I had in a very long time. I asked if she would accompany me into town, for I wanted to get a photograph taken of us together, and she said she would be delighted. The carriage took us to a photographer's studio, where I was amused to see an image of my own self as a Circassian Girl for sale along with many other *carte de visites* of friends, present and past.[54]

As he took our picture,[55] the photographer spoke of how excited he was to get to the show after the work day was over and asked if we planned on attending. I smiled to think he had a performer from that very show whose picture was in his gallery right in front of him and didn't even know it. Grandmother asked what the fuss was about.

I leaned down and asked her, "Have you ever been to the circus?"

---

[54] It was common practice for photography studios to sell images of famous people, from presidents to sideshow performers. The photos in my own family album that led me to the mistaken conclusion that my ancestors were sideshow performers probably came from a studio like the one Zara stopped in with her grandmother. Funny that it never occurred to me while reading Zara's book as a kid that there could have been another reason for those photos to be in our album. I guess we believe what we want to believe.

[55] Sarah M. also had a copy of this photo. In the real-world version, the little old woman in the chair does indeed wear clothes out of fashion for the time, but of threadbare cotton, not silk and lace. Zara's skin appears darker here than in any of her photos as a Circassian Beauty—one wonders if those professional photos were exposed or developed to give her skin a lighter appearance—but though she does appear much lighter than the old woman, the family resemblance is striking. Zara stands behind, a hand on her grandmother's shoulder. Sarah, who Zara was named for, reaches up to hold that hand. Both are beaming. For portraiture of the time, the image is unusually alive.

CHAPTER SEVEN

LOVE HEALS ALL WOUNDS—THE PRINCESS MARRIES
HER PRINCE—AN HEIR TO THE THRONE—A FAIRY
TALE COMES TO AN END

I pushed Grandmother all over the midway in her chair, describing the sights for her. Despite the state of her vision, Grandmother declared the show to be the most marvelous thing she had ever seen. She had never heard a parrot screech or a tiger roar before, and she had certainly never seen a girl in a tiny costume walk a tightrope or somersault through the air to be caught in the arms of a man in spangled tights. The vendors called out their wares as children ran by laughing and sweethearts giggled, arm in arm. I realized I hadn't actually *seen* the show since that first time, when I snuck in inside my father's cart, the Athenian Siren on my lap.

I took Grandmother inside the tent where the Strong Man was performing. As he glowered and growled his way through the performance, his eyes found Grandmother and me in the crowd. Forgetting the act for just a moment, he smiled.

The barker stumbled to explain. "There," he stammered. "He is thinking of his love, even now!"

I leaned down to Grandmother. "I'm going to marry him," I told her.

"That beast?" she asked, then patted my hand. "Good."

After I had brought Grandmother home, the carriage driver raced to get me back to the show before it began the move to the next town. I made it to the train just as the wheels began to turn. At once I sought out the Strong Man, and once again we did not need words. My sorrow healed, I fell into his arms.

The next day, we broke the news of our intent to marry to our circus family and were met with a great cheer. The Showman declared that he would have a notice printed in the local paper of the next town announcing our impending nuptials, and we were happy to contribute a little publicity to the endeavour of the man who had brought us together.[56]

The Showman had a new act in mind for us. The tailor was brought in and a new costume created overnight for the Circassian Prince who had travelled the world over and finally found his betrothed. The Prince had been enraged to learn of my marriage to the Englishman, but had softened when he learned of the loss of my child, and was understanding of how helpless a beautiful and mesmerizing woman in a strange land was to find her way home unaccompanied and unscathed. I had so beseeched him with my eyes alone that I had no need to resort to the use of the talents I was taught in preparation for my sale to the sultan's palace, the sale that had been thwarted by the Showman's wily agent. Now that we were reunited, we could soon return to take our seats at the throne of our homeland together. In the meantime, I was teaching him English.

Covering up his previously skimpily clad fine form with silks in colours that matched my own and topping his now clean and

---

[56] And then some—announcements that the wedding was to take place at the show in THAT VERY TOWN appeared in every local newspaper for the duration of the tour, though a marriage record cannot be found in any of them. Did the couple ever marry? If so, Zara's first marriage wouldn't have been over until the death of her first husband in 1893 (that is, if I have located the correct Richard Hughes), so a second marriage wouldn't have been a legal one, anyhow. Perhaps she was following in her parents' unconventional tradition of commitment being as good as law.

combed black hair with a fur hat helped to convince the audience that the Prince was not the former Strong Man or Wild Man of the Tundra. As the tour came to a close we were as popular an act as we had ever been, and I was carrying his child. We returned for a time to the apartment in the city. We knew not what we would do next, but it seemed that now we had found our way to each other, our performing days had ended. We had lived our adventures and made more than enough money to retire right then and live quite comfortably. All we wanted now was to quietly and happily raise our family.

I sold the shop to Father's clerk, packed up the belongings in the apartment, and we moved to a modest but modern house not far from the cabin where I had grown up. The baby came soon after, a healthy boy. Though it was the happiest time in my life, it was marred by the news that Grandmother had finally passed. I felt fortunate to have the bittersweet memory of our day at the circus and the photo of us together to comfort me.

My Prince accompanied me to the funeral, which was attended by even more people than that of my own father. I was humbled by all the members of prominent families who came to pay their respects, and met many family members whose names I had never even known.[57]

---

[57] While the first part of that statement is likely fiction, if she did in fact attend, the second part is surely fact. While the question of Gaby's paternity will likely never be resolved, Wilma's family's oral history has it that her biological father was a slave owner and that Gaby was the result of a secret affair, rape, or a blurred combination of the two. Zara's account of Gaby being turned out of the house has it that her aristocratic father disapproved of her penniless Jewish husband. The hardness of Gaby's father towards her could back up either theory, but the former seems more likely. Did Zara

As we travelled home, my Prince was afflicted with a persistent cough. He made light of it, suggesting he merely had a touch of the ague, would take some bed rest and soon be well again. But by the time we reached home, he was shivering with fever and beginning to lose his senses. I called for a doctor, but in the country, help does not come so fast as it does in the city. By the time the physician arrived it was dawn, and I had been up all night caring for my Prince.

The doctor, the same old man who had attended the birth of one of my sisters, performed an examination and released a heavy breath before turning to face me. I moaned, knowing what he would say—our happiness was coming to an end. There was nothing more to do than stay by my Prince.

I brought our son to the bedside and kept my Prince as comfortable as I could, soothing his brow, singing to him, his hand in mine. He grew less and less restless and finally slept like a baby, cheeks flushed with fever.

I awoke at his bedside, my head upon his breast, to feel his hand slipping from mine. I kissed the smile that played at his lips in death as I wept. Our child toddled to me and reached up. I pulled him into my arms.

"Don't cry," he said. "Don't cry. Daddy has gone to the circus."

I laughed through my tears. "Yes, my darling, he has."[58]

---

know about the possibility that her biological grandfather was not the man who raised her mother when (and if) she attended her grandmother's funeral? Was Gaby's father's hardness toward Gaby shared by other family members? If Zara had been aware of this rejection, could it have kept her away from the funeral? Or, on the occasion of her grandmother's death, was the family ready to be brought together again? Was Ivan the Great really there with their child? If so, what did the family think of them both?

[58] This bit of repeated narrative absolutely thrilled me as a boy, but as an adult with a much more speculative eye on the author's reliability, I'm still so damn fond of Zara that I'm reluctant to impugn the talents of my subject and suggest it seems a hackneyed device. Instead, I'll address the topic of the second child.

It should not surprise you to learn I've been unable to find a record of this birth. We do know there was a son, natural or not, who carried on the family line; the existence of Sarah M. is proof of that. Oral history passed down though the family includes detailed early memories that Zara's son retained of Ivan. Now, if the second child was conceived during Putnam's tour of 1871 (the year the train derailed and the first son was lost) and the tour ended in October of the same year, and the second baby was born before Zara's grandmother died in November of 1872 (Wilma's information makes it possible to confirm this), then Ivan came down with the illness that would kill him on the way home from that same funeral, that second baby would have been an infant at the time of his father's death, which makes his later recollection of Ivan teaching him to whistle with a blade of grass not only an incredible feat of recall, but an advanced display of early motor skills as well.

But suppose that first child, stolen away by his father in the night, then abandoned at an orphanage, had been relocated and reclaimed by his mother upon moving back to the country. This move could have been, in fact, made with the very purpose of finding the child in mind. That child—Baby Beethoven/Wolfgang—would then have been about seven years old when Ivan died. Old enough to have memories of Ivan into adulthood, and old enough to remember that when Mommy was crying, talk of the circus could make her laugh. Keep this in mind as you read on.

CHAPTER EIGHT

A LIFE IN REFLECTION—A NEW PRINCE AND
PRINCESS—ONE TRUE LOVE—RUNNING OFF TO THE
CIRCUS—A TINY BEAUTY—LIGHT IN THE DARKNESS

Many years have passed since my performing days, and, though I do not regret my retirement one bit, I often look back on those days with great fondness and yearn to see those faces once more. The Giantess passed away nearly half my lifetime ago, and the armless lady, who so consoled me with her friendship many years after the rest had gone, is only a memory now. A Tattooed Lady whom I met only after I left the show became a wonderful source of companionship and provided me with endless bawdy tales and potent nips of fine Georgian brandy, but she too has passed into history. And my Prince—even today I ache to see his glowering gaze transform into a smile as our eyes meet. In memory, he is forever in the bloom of his youth. He would not recognize his Princess now, hair gone white and hands gnarled with age. Though I have been pursued by many since his death, I have remained true to my one and only Prince.

Our son proved to be gifted at music, as my own father and mother were.[59]

He was a natural scholar, as well, so I filled the house with books for him to devour. He could be a kind and attentive child, but had a beastly side, and once he was old enough to take an interest in the fairer sex, I struggled to understand his moods and keep him happy.[60]

---

[59] As was Professor Hughs.

[60] The son's temperament seems much more similar in nature to that of the

In college he met a girl from a prestigious family who seemed to tame the beast in him, and it wasn't long before they were engaged to be married. The wedding was a grand affair, and every prominent American name was accounted for at the reception when the bride and groom took to the floor for their first dance.[61]

Upon his graduation, my son became a professor of music[62] and was in part responsible for many a distinguished symphony conductor and performer. He and his charming wife have several children, the youngest of whom, a girl, has inherited my unruly curls in combination with my son's auburn colour, rendering her quite striking.[63]

Before age overtook me, and my son and daughter-in-law kindly brought me to live at their home, I would, on occasion, under oath of secrecy, take my granddaughter to the circus, which she delighted in. I pointed out humbuggery to her where I saw it, never letting on how I had gleaned that knowledge. In part this was due to the wishes of my son, who wanted my former occupation kept secret, but I had no burning desire to tell her all,

---

charming but explosive Professor than that of the glowering but gentle giant, Ivan.

[61] Confirmed through Sarah M.'s documentation and historical events— Zara's circus child, likely descended from slaves, counted among his wedding guests the aristocratic descendants of many owners of slaves.

[62] !!!

[63] Professor Hughs, the "Lion of Carnarvon," was distinguished by his shock of red hair. Ivan, whether of Russian, Spanish, or some other nationality, had decidedly dark hair, and, of course, Zara herself had black hair.

The granddaughter described here is the mother of Sarah M.

at least not then. One day, I thought, I would write a book and she could read all about who I had been. In the meantime, I encouraged her to dig through my old Turkish costumes and play her own games with them, the fiery curls that would shame any Circassian Beauty streaming about her head as she enacted whatever role struck her fancy.

My eyes fail me with more frequency now, and my hand sometimes aches to hold the pen, but every day I seem to remember more clearly the friends I held so dear and the family lost too soon. I cherish every moment and do not fear tomorrow, for I know my Prince is waiting to meet me under the Big Top, that secret smile upon his lips.

AFTERWORD

Zara passed away in the home of her son and daughter-in-law thirteen months after completing this book. Of the voluminous and priceless gifts from royals and dignitaries given to her, none have survived. Only the family photos and letters, now in possession of her great-granddaughter, Sarah M., are known to still exist.

ABOUT THE ANNOTATOR

Joshua Chapman Green is the youngest child of a sort of Jewish father and somewhat African-American mother, neither of whom thought any of that mattered, and maybe it doesn't, but maybe it does. He lives in southern Ohio with his wife, her infinite patience, and three dogs that followed him home. His hobbies include writing books about people who'd rather be left alone and searching for clues to mysteries that can probably never be solved.